# Farm Boy Series

# Tomatoes

## Cindy Palumbo

Illustrated by Ryan Brady

Archway Publishing books may be ordered through booksellers or by contacting:

Archway Publishing
1663 Liberty Drive
Bloomington, IN 47403
www.archwaypublishing.com
1 (888) 242-5904

ISBN: 978-1-4808-2098-2 (sc)
ISBN: 978-1-4808-2099-9 (hc)
ISBN: 978-1-4808-2100-2 (e)

Library of Congress Control Number: 2015949699

Print information available on the last page.

Archway Publishing rev. date: 9/22/2015

Farm Boy Series

# Tomatoes

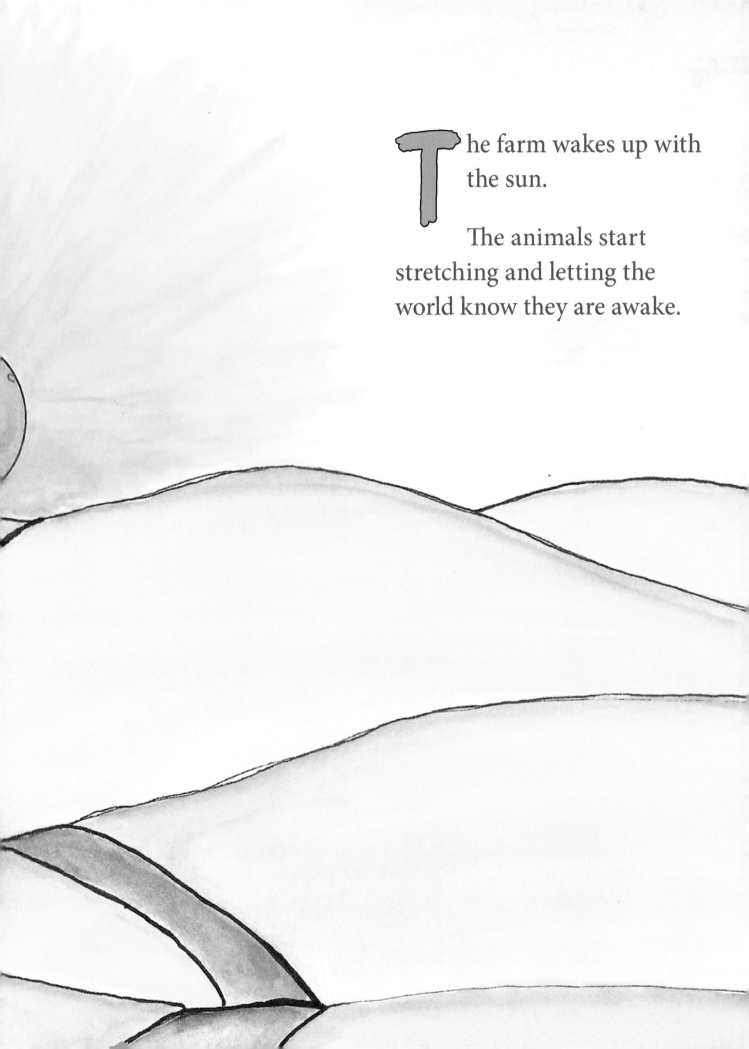

The farm wakes up with the sun.

The animals start stretching and letting the world know they are awake.

Dominick is barely rolling out of bed when he hears his Mom call to him.

"Rise and Shine my little farmer, today we are planting tomatoes."

Dominick doesn't want to get up, he doesn't want to plant tomatoes, he doesn't like tomatoes.

"Come on Dominick, if we are going to have tomatoes in the summer, we need to plant them now."

He pulls on his jeans, his boots and heads downstairs.

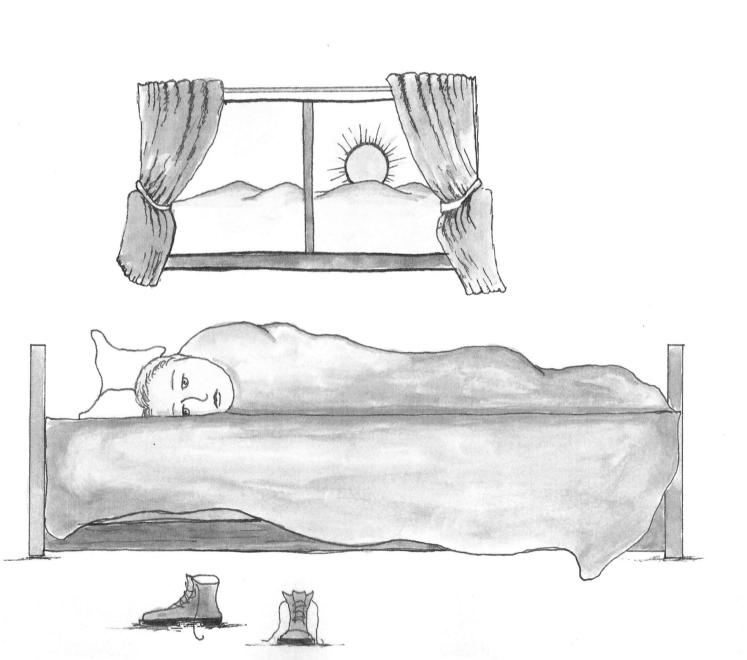

Breakfast is waiting. Oatmeal, fruit and juice, his favorite.

"Eat up and let's get going before it gets too hot", says his Mom.

Dominick's Dad was already out on the
tractor. He was mowing the grass in the
vineyard.

Dominick would rather be on the tractor
with his Dad. He follows his mom out to the
animal coral and they feed and water the
goats, chickens, turkeys and pigs.

They head over to the garden.

They start by digging holes in a row, 2 feet apart.

"Now put a little plant in each hole and gently cover it up", said Dominick's Mom.

Dominick is bored, "I don't like tomatoes!"

"You will like these, they are better when you have done the work and grown them yourself" says his Mom.

They planted all the little seedlings and gave each one water.

Dominick watched the tomatoes…
March ended, April began.

He kept watering the little plants and
they were growing, but it was so slow.
Dominick was getting impatient, it
was taking too long.

"These plants will never grow tomatoes, they are just green plants, not red tomatoes", he told his Mom.

His mom stated, "They are growing, keep visiting them each day, make sure the weeds are pulled around them and keep those worms off of the plants. They will grow beautiful red tomatoes."

"I don't even like tomatoes", Dominick reminded his Mom.

The month of May came
and went and it rained
and rained and rained.

Dominick kept checking
the tomatoes. The plants
were getting bigger and
they had little yellow
flowers on them. He
made sure he pulled the
worms off every day.

June and July arrived, it was summer and Dominick loved summer. He started noticing that the little flowers had turned to little green balls, like tiny marbles. He kept watering the plants, pulling weeds and picking off any worms. The plants had grown as tall as Dominick and he remembered how little they were when they were first planted. Dominick was proud of the work he had done. Although he was excited to see the little tomatoes change from green to red, Dominick remembered that he still didn't like tomatoes.

One Saturday morning Dominick was waking up slow and he heard his mom call to him.

"Rise and Shine sleepy head, I have something to show you".

Dominick came running down the stairs, he had a feeling that this was going to be a great day.

They headed out to the garden and his mom told him to look at his plants.

He couldn't believe what he saw, it looked like a giant bouquet of plump, red balloons were hanging on to the plant.

His plants had big, beautiful, bright red tomatoes all over. "Here is a basket, why don't you pick the ones that are red" said his Mom. "There are so many, what are we going to do with so many?" Dominick replied. "Why don't you try one?" She said Dominick reminded his mom that he didn't like tomatoes. "Just try one!"

He took one of the small, bright red tomatoes and rubbed it on his pants to wipe off any dirt. Here goes nothing, he thought and popped it into his mouth. It was amazing, it was sweet and juicy and tasted as sweet as summer. A giant smile came across his face.

"They taste a lot better when you have done all the hard work to grow them, don't they?" said his Mom.

"Oh yes" replied Dominick, "I know what we can do with them. Let's make spaghetti sauce, put them on salads and sandwiches. We can put them on everything!"

He was so excited, he didn't want to drop one single tomato. He remembered how long ago he and his Mom had planted them. He remembered the months of hard work to keep the weeds pulled and the worms off and to keep his plants watered. Now they were here and every single tomato had his hard work in it and Dominick wasn't going to waste a single one.

Dominick realized why it was important not to waste food, he realized how much work went into growing a single tomato. He realized how good he felt about growing food for his family.

Dominick realized, he liked tomatoes.

CPSIA information can be obtained at www.ICGtesting.com
Printed in the USA
LVOW05*1932290915

456225LV00011B/72/P